Too Many Books!

Written by Gilles Tibo  Illustrated by Bruno St-Aubin

Scholastic Canada Ltd.

Toronto New York London Auckland Sydney
Mexico City New Delhi Hong Kong Buenos Aires

Scholastic Canada Ltd.
175 Hillmount Road, Markham, Ontario L6C 1Z7, Canada

Scholastic Inc.
555 Broadway, New York, NY 10012, USA

Scholastic Australia Pty Limited
PO Box 579, Gosford, NSW 2250, Australia

Scholastic New Zealand Limited
Private Bag 94407, Greenmount, Auckland, New Zealand

Scholastic Ltd.
Villiers House, Clarendon Avenue, Leamington Spa,
Warwickshire CV32 5PR, UK

National Library of Canada Cataloguing in Publication

Tibo, Gilles, 1951-
[Des livres pour Nicolas!. English]
Too many books! / Gilles Tibo ; illustrated by Bruno St-Aubin ;
translated by Petra Johannson.

Translation of: Des livres pour Nicolas!

ISBN 0-439-96753-8

I. St-Aubin, Bruno II. Johannson, Petra III. Title. IV. Title:
Des livres pour Nicolas!. English.

PS8589.I26D4813 2004   jC843'.54   C2003-905181-1

Translation by Petra Johannson
Text copyright © 2003 by Gilles Tibo
Illustrations copyright © 2003 by Bruno St-Aubin
English text copyright © 2004 by Scholastic Canada Ltd.
All rights reserved.

6 5 4 3 2 1   Printed in Canada   04 05 06 07 08

One morning, Nicholas got dressed in a hurry and ran downstairs to find his mom. She gave him a hug, took one look at his shoelaces and said, "Nicholas, I have something for you."

Then she searched through a box and handed him a book about how to tie shoelaces.

4

After Nicholas read it, he could tie the best bows in the world.

5

When he finished his breakfast, he brushed his teeth very fast

VVVRRRiiiOOOUUUMMM!

Toothpaste flew all over the bathroom.

His dad ran in, gave him a kiss, and handed him another book – on how to brush your teeth.

BLUB! BLUB! BLUB!

After Nicholas read it, he had the whitest, brightest teeth in the world.

Then he tried to give his cat a bath. She did not want one.

His sister appeared, holding a book in her hands. Oh no!
Not a book about how to wash cats!

After Nicholas read it, his cat was the cleanest, most beautiful cat in the world.

13

Nicholas decided to go outside and play. He tried riding his bike. It wasn't easy.

His favourite neighbour, Veronica, came over with a book under her arm.

"No!" said Nicholas. "You must be kidding! Not a book about how to ride like a pro!"

After Nicholas read it, he was the best bike rider in the world.

To thank Veronica, Nicholas went to the library with her. The minute they got there, she dove straight for the shelves and chose a stack of books.

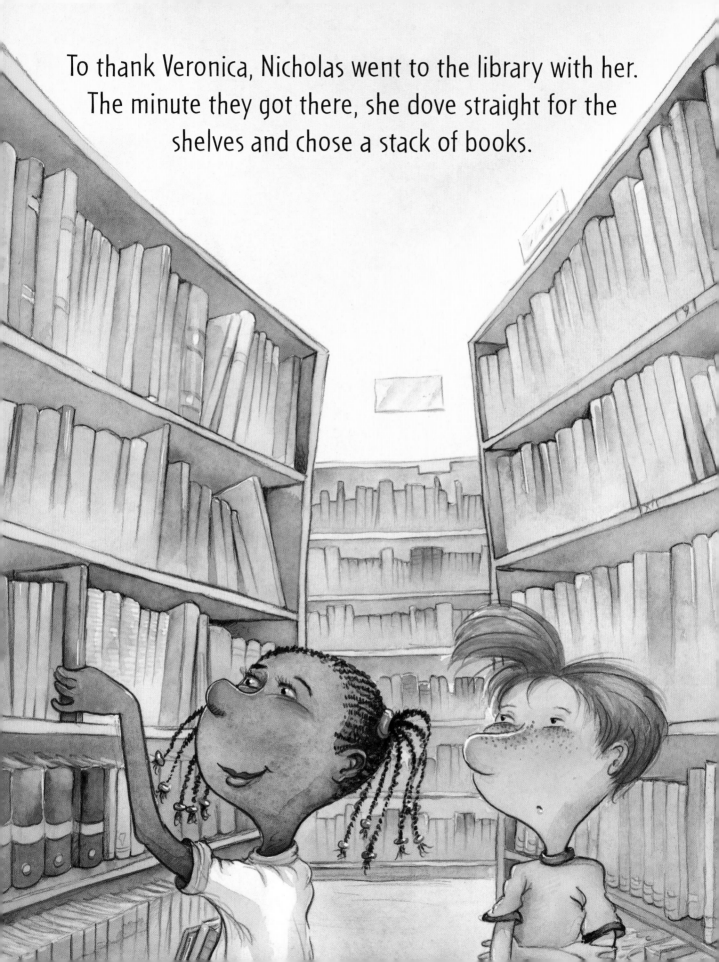

Hugging her pile, she asked Nicholas, "Aren't you getting any?"

"No!" said Nicholas. "I'm tired of reading books that tell me how to do this, how to do that... how not to do this, how not to do that..."

Veronica grabbed him by the hand. "Look, Nicholas! Over here are adventures. Over there you'll find history. And down this row are the funny books."

To make her happy, Nicholas chose three – a pirate adventure, a book about knights and a funny story.

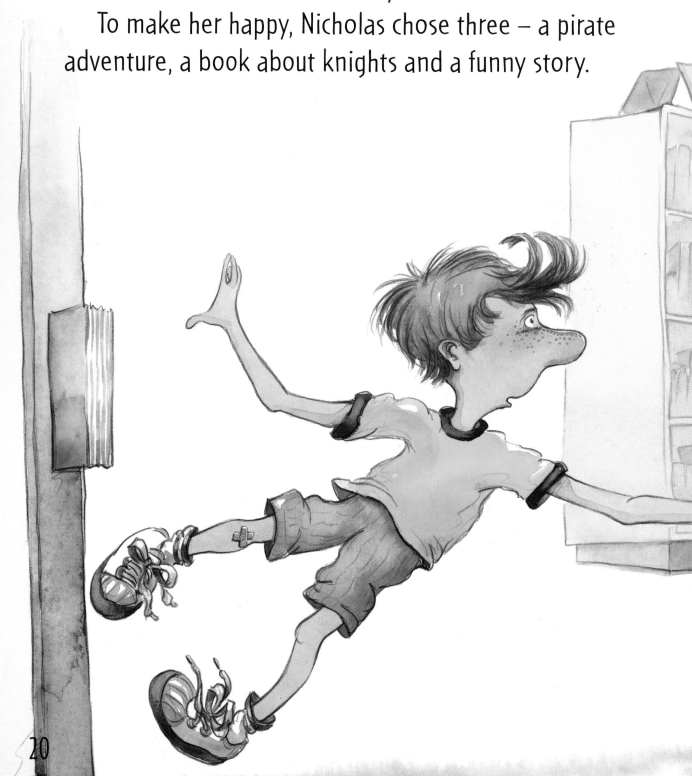

21

On the way back, Veronica kept saying, "I can't wait to read my books!"

"Um…uh…me, too…I can hardly wait…" said Nicholas.

At home, he headed to the backyard to play,
plunking his books on the grass. Hmm, he thought.
Should he give one of them a try?

Nicholas sat down under the tree, opened the funny book and started to read. He burst out laughing on the first page. And on the second page...
And the third...

He laughed so hard that his dad opened the back door and asked, "What's going on, Nicholas?"

His mom came out of the garage and asked, "Nicholas, are you all right?"

Then his dad, his mom, his sister and Veronica all gathered around. With a big smile, Nicholas said, "Listen to this – 'Once there was a little mouse who…'"

After Nicholas finished, he was the happiest reader in the world!